A Feel Better Book

for Little
Poopers

To our own little poopers — we love you so stinkin' much. — HB & LB

To the reader and to caregivers: my sincerest wishes that this story provides support in the bathroom department, and a smile here and there! It was a joy to illustrate this book, thank you Holly, Leah, and the team at Magination Press/APA! — SN-B

Books for Kids From the
American Psychological Association

Magination Press is a registered trademark of the American Psychological Association. Order books at maginationpress.org, or call 1-800-374-2721.

Book design by Gwen Grafft
Printed by Worzalla, Stevens Point, WI

Cataloguing-in-Publication data is on file at the Library of Congress.
ISBN-13: 978-1-4338-3240-6
LCCN: 2019049977

Manufactured in the United States of America
10 9 8 7 6 5 4 3 2 1

A Feel Better Book

for Little Poopers

by Holly Brochmann and Leah Bowen

illustrated by Shirley Ng-Benitez

MAGINATION PRESS · WASHINGTON, DC
American Psychological Association

The sun is shining,
it's a beautiful day.
Your friends are all waiting
to go out and play.

But something has stopped you
from joining the group...
oh no, not again!
You have to go poop!

You don't want to go
in the potty like you should—
you're worried and scared
that it won't feel good.

So you're holding it in
for as long as you can.
You're missing the fun,
it's wrecking your plans!

Now your tummy is hurting,
you're stuck on the couch.
This problem is turning
you into a grouch.

You think it's coming!
You scream and you shout,
just please, oh please
DON'T LET THAT POOP OUT!

It's very confusing
when your head says no
but your body is saying
I really need to go!

But you don't have to let
poop ruin your day.
You'll be happy to hear
there's an easier way!

You just need to learn
some new tricks and tactics.
Like anything else
it takes patience and practice.

So bid farewell to your fear,
tell your worries goodbye!
It gets better from here—
now you're ready to try!

First relax your body;
take some deep breaths in,
then let them all out
before you begin.

Now let's imagine
you're holding a rock.
It's heavy in your arms
and it's too hard to walk.

Throw that rock in a lake!
Listen to it drop.
It lands in the water
with a splash and a plop!

Just like that rock,
poop weighs you down.
So letting go is better
than carrying it around.

If it's still hard to go,
there's more we can try.
Put your feet on a stool
and bring your knees up high.

Sitting this way,
in the shape of a squat,
helps it come out
and go into the pot.

And sometimes it helps
to sit at the same time
every morning and night
while repeating this rhyme:

"I know I can do this!
I'm brave and I'm strong!
Soon I'll feel better
and can play all day long!"

Superheroes, princesses,
presidents and mayors,
firefighters, dancers,
and basketball players…

Everyone has to
spend time on the potty.
Believe you can do it,
just trust in your body!

Whether the potty's at home,
a friend's house, or school,
you can let that poop out.
There's really no rule!

When poop has to come
your body knows what to do.
It's just part of life
and you will make it through.

You're feeling quite ready,
there's nothing to fear!
So come on and let's get it
STINKY in here!!

Note to Parents and Caregivers

A *Feel Better Book for Little Poopers* is intended to address the anxiety that can happen when children are scared to have a bowel movement, which usually begins during or soon after potty training. There is a common, but vicious cycle that happens when a child is scared to use the bathroom — they hold their poop in, subsequently become constipated, it hurts when it finally does come out, the pain creates fear so they hold it again, and the cycle is repeated over and over. Our goal for this book is to help break that cycle by easing the child's fears and creating a routine of using the potty.

However, if your child consistently has trouble going, it is important to first discuss the situation with your pediatrician to rule out any underlying health issues, sensory sensitivities, or diet concerns. Our bodies are usually very good at signaling when something is wrong, and "poop problems" can mean something is going on that we should pay attention to.

You're worried and scared that it won't feel good. Poop can be a fun and silly topic for children, one that they (and many adults even!) like to make jokes about. But for anyone who has experienced a child who holds their bowels, it is anything but funny. The fear is real, and it is profound. To us as adults, it may seem so simple, but for young kids it is very new. Children of potty-training age have been wearing a diaper since the very moment they were born. The transition to sitting on a cold, hard chair in a position that is often not advantageous for the release of bowels can be not only scary, but physically difficult. When they do go, it feels strange to them, and it becomes an experience they are not eager to repeat. The fear can be even more intense for older children who have had painful movements in the past. As a caregiver, it is important to provide comfort, compassion and patience during this learning process, and understand that it might take longer than what is advertised with potty training. It is also very helpful to acknowledge what they are going through, but provide assurance that it will get better. For example you can say, "You're new at this and it just takes time." Or "I know it hurt last time and you're scared it's going to hurt again, but together we will practice some new things to try that can help."

You're missing the fun, it's wrecking your plans. This is one of the worst consequences of that vicious cycle. Your child needs to poop, but they are scared and seek control by avoidance (holding it in). When they finally reach a point when they have no choice but to go (sometimes days later!), it's hard and it hurts, validating all their fears. In between, the child becomes very uncomfortable and grouchy—in some cases, they miss out on playtime, family outings, school activities, etc. But there really isn't a way to force your child to go. This is extremely frustrating for caregivers, and it often leads to putting pressure on your child to go. But pressuring your child or shaming them for feeling scared will only intensify the fear, making matters worse. Instead, you can reflect their feelings with gentle statements such as, "You're worried it will hurt, but it doesn't feel good holding it in, either." Or "Listen to your body, and when you're ready to give it a try I'll be here with you." When you have plans and need to be somewhere or do something, it is *hard* to not put any pressure on your child. Remind yourself that your child is not doing this out of spite but out of fear, and they need you right now.

It's very confusing when your head says no but your body is saying I really need to go! There can be an internal struggle when the child knows they need to go to the bathroom and sit and try, but their fear stops them! This is why it helps to talk to the child about listening to your body's signals, and how by paying attention you can give your body what it needs to work like it should. You can show them a diagram of the intestines, and explain how poop moves through the body and is stored in the colon until it gets full enough to come out. A good visual demonstration of this is filling a balloon with water. As more water flows into the balloon, it gets fuller and fuller until it has no choice but to start coming out of the top (try not to let the balloon pop, as that could scare the child!).

First relax your body, take some deep breaths in. Like with most things, relaxation helps. But this is easier said than done when your child is stressed. Try starting mindfulness practices like deep breathing at times when they are calm, such as before bedtime, when sitting on the couch together, etc. That way when your child is feeling panicked, they will already have it down and will know what to do! Also, as a caregiver who is potentially feeling frustrated and impatient, it is equally, if not

more, important for you to remember to take deep breaths, too. When your child agrees to try to potty, stay calm and model deep breathing techniques.

Sitting this way, in the shape of a squat helps it come out and go into the pot. This suggestion can help your child in two different ways. First, research and testimonials have shown that the squatting position can physically help poop come out easier, as it places the body in a more natural position for a bowel movement. But perhaps equally important, it is an element of the process that the child can elect to do differently and therefore control. Giving them something physical to try is often easier than changing their mindset. You can further engage the child by offering to let them decorate their potty stool in a special way, or give it a clever name.

Trust in your body, everyone has to spend time on the potty! While normalizing the child's need to poop — it's something every person, animal, and insect does! — it's also

important to acknowledge that it's okay to be afraid, and that they're not the only one who experiences this fear. Lots of kids, and even adults for that matter, feel scared when they are learning something new or are nervous because they experienced hardship in the past. But that feeling inside is your body telling you that you need to poop — which means your body is working like it should!

You're feeling quite ready, there's nothing to fear! Caregivers of a child who holds their poop probably feel almost as much relief as the child when they finally go! Celebrate their bravery! Reflect their feelings with a "you did it!" or "You were scared but you listened to your body!" Be sure to give encouragement even when they don't quite make it. "You had an accident but you sure did try!"

In closing, one of the main things to remember as a parent or caregiver when your child withholds their bowel movements is to stay calm. Putting more pressure on your child *will not help*. This can be so difficult to do when frustration levels are high, so much of this process involves mindfulness and preparation practices by the caregiver. Have patience with yourself; you may not always respond the way you wish you would have. Forgive yourself and explain to your child that you are learning, too. We hope this book will help you talk with them about these fears and help them feel more comfortable giving it a try.

About the Authors

Sisters LEAH BOWEN and HOLLY BROCHMANN are dedicated wives, mothers, and authors, each passionate about contributing to a mentally and emotionally healthier society in a meaningful way. Leah has a master of education degree in counseling with a focus in play therapy. She is a licensed professional counselor and registered play therapist in the state of Texas where she currently practices, and she is committed to helping her child clients work through issues including trauma, depression, and anxiety. Holly has a degree in journalism and enjoys creative writing both as a hobby and as a primary part of her career in public relations. This is the sisters' fourth book in the Feel Better Books for Little Kids series published by Magination Press. Both sisters live in Texas. Visit www.bsistersbooks.com.

About the Illustrator

SHIRLEY NG-BENITEZ loves to draw and write! As an award-winning illustrator, Shirley's honored to have illustrated over twenty books for children, including the three other books in the Feel Better Books for Little Kids series. She works in watercolors, gouache, colored pencil, and digital finishing, and is always trying new techniques. She's the owner of gabbyandco.com, a design/illustration/lettering firm, lives in the San Francisco Bay area with her family and two kittens, and is currently writing and illustrating her own stories for children. For more, please visit shirleyngbenitez.com and visit Shirley on Twitter and Instagram @shirleysillos.

About Magination Press

MAGINATION PRESS is the children's book imprint of the American Psychological Association. Through APA's publications, the association shares with the world mental health expertise and psychological knowledge. Magination Press books reach young readers and their parents and caregivers to make navigating life's challenges a little easier. It's the combined power of psychology and literature that makes a Magination Press book special. Visit www.maginationpress.org.